To ....

For being good.

MERRY CHRISTMAS!

From Santa

Santa is coming to San Francisco

Written by Steve Smallman
Illustrated by Robert Dunn
Designed by Sarah Allen

Published by Sourcebooks Jabberwocky, an imprint of Sourcebooks, Inc.
P.O. Box 4410, Naperville, Illinois 60567-4410
(630) 961-3900
Fax: (630) 961-2168
www.jabberwockykids.com

Library of Congress Cataloging-in-Publication data is on file with the publisher.

Source of Production: Leo Paper Products, Guangdong Province, China
Date of Production: April 2014
Run Number: HTW_PO170314
Printed and bound in China
LEO 10 9 8 7 6 5 4 3

Santa is coming to San Francisco

Written by Steve Smallman

Illustrated by Robert Dunn

sourcebooks
jabberwocky

"Well?"

boomed Santa. "Have all the children from **San Francisco** been good this year?"

"Well...uh...mostly," answered the little old elf, as he bustled across the busy workshop to Santa's desk.

Santa peered down at the elf from behind the tall, teetering piles of letters that the children of San Francisco had sent him.

"Mostly?" asked Santa, looking over the top of his glasses.

"Yes...but they've all been **especially** good in the last few days!" said the elf.

"Jolly good!" chuckled Santa,
"Then we'd better get their presents loaded up!"

Even though the sack of presents was

really, really big

and the elves were really, really small,

they seemed to have no trouble loading it onto Santa's sleigh.
Though how they managed to fit such a big sack into one little sleigh
even they didn't know. But somehow they did.

"Splendid!" boomed Santa. "We're ready to go!"

"Er...not quite, Santa," said the little old elf. "One of our reindeer is missing!"

"Missing?

Which reindeer is missing?" asked Santa.

"The youngest one, Santa," said the elf. "It's his first flight tonight. I've called him and called him, but..."

Just then, a young reindeer strolled up, munching on a large carrot.

"Where have you been?"

asked Santa.

But the youngest reindeer was crunching so loudly that it was no wonder he hadn't heard the little old elf calling.

"Oh well, never mind," said Santa, giving the reindeer a little wink.
He took out his Santa-nav and tapped in the coordinates for San Francisco.
"This will guide us to San Francisco in no time."

Crunch!
Crunch!
Crunch!

With a flick of the reins and a jerk of the harness, off they went, racing through the sky.

"Ho, ho, ho!"
laughed Santa.

"We'll soon have these presents
delivered to the City by the Bay!"

Santa's sleigh flew through the starry night, heading south across the Arctic Ocean. On they flew in the wintry air, crossing over the Sierra Nevada. In the wink of an eye, the sleigh was flying across Sacramento and on over Walnut Creek. The youngest reindeer was very excited. He had never been away from the North Pole before.

They had just crossed San Francisco Bay
when, suddenly, they ran into a thick fog.
Mist swirled around the sleigh.

They couldn't see a thing!

The youngest reindeer was getting a bit worried,
but Santa didn't seem concerned.

"In two miles..."

said the Santa-nav in a bossy lady's voice,

"...keep left at the next star."

"But, ma'am," Santa blustered, "I can't see any stars in all this fog!"
Soon they were

hopelessly lost!

Bong-bong!
Bong-bong!

Then, through the swirling fog, the youngest reindeer heard a faint, chiming sound.

Bong-bong!

He looked over at the old reindeer with the red nose. But he had his head down.

(Red nose...I wonder who that could be?!)

Bong-bong
Bong-bong!

Bong-bong!
Bong-bong!

There was that sound again, like a clock chiming. The youngest reindeer turned around to look at Santa. But Santa wasn't listening. He seemed to be arguing with a little box with buttons on it.

With a flick of the harness and a jerk of the reins, the youngest reindeer gave a sharp *tug* and headed off toward the sound of the bells, pulling Santa and his sleigh behind him!

"Whoa!"

cried Santa, pulling his hat straight.
"What's going on?" Then, to his surprise,
he heard the chiming sound.

"Well done, young reindeer!" he shouted
cheerfully, "It must be the Ferry Building clock.
Don't worry, children, Santa is coming!"

Then, suddenly...

CRUNCH!

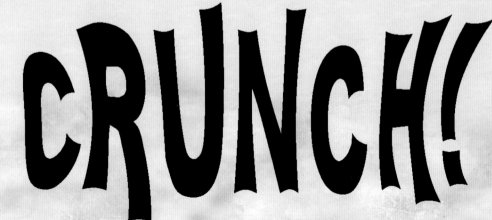

The sleigh hit something as it plummeted through the fog,
"You have arrived!"
said the Santa-nav unhelpfully.

Finally, when the fog had lifted, Santa discovered exactly where they were...

...stuck, right at the very top of the tower at Alcatraz!

"Everybody, PULL!"

The reindeer *pulled* with all their might until, at last, with a screeching noise, the sleigh scraped clear of the Alcatraz tower and Santa steered them safely past Coit Tower, above the Civic Center, over the Japanese Tea Garden, and down into Golden Gate Park.

Luckily, there was no
real damage done, but
the packages had all been
jumbled up. Santa quickly sorted
the presents into order again.

"All right," said Santa. "Thanks to this
young reindeer I know where we are
now. Don't worry, children,

Santa is coming!"

Santa drove his sleigh expertly from rooftop to rooftop all over San Francisco, popping in and out of chimneys as fast as he could go.

(which was pretty fast for a chubby fellow!)

There were big chimneys in Richmond, and small chimneys in Japantown. He squeezed down thin chimneys in Noe Valley, and plummeted down fat chimneys in Nob Hill.

The youngest reindeer was amazed at how quickly they went. Santa never seemed to get tired at all! And it looked like the children in San Francisco were going to be very lucky this year! But the youngest reindeer was starting to feel a bit weary and quite hungry too!

He piled them under the Christmas trees
and carefully filled up the stockings
with surprises.

In house after house, Santa delved
inside his sack for packages of
every shape and size.

Santa took a little bite out of each cookie, a tiny sip of milk, wiped his beard, and popped the carrots into his sack.

In house after house, the good children of San Francisco had left out a plate of cookies, a small glass of milk, and a big, crunchy carrot.

From Berkeley to Pacific Heights, from Corte Madera to Chinatown, from Oakland to the Sunset District, and ALL the places in between, Santa and his sleigh visited every house in San Francisco.

Finally, Santa had delivered the
last present on his long San Francisco list.

"Great moons and stars!" sighed
Santa. "It's past midnight and my sack seems as
heavy as ever! I hope I haven't forgotten anyone."

Santa opened his sack to check...but it was full
of juicy, crunchy carrots!

Santa divided the carrots among all the reindeer.
"Well, done!" he said, patting the youngest reindeer gently on the nose.

But the youngest reindeer didn't hear him...
he was too busy munching!

Then it was time to set off for home. Santa reset his Santa-nav
once more to the North Pole, and soon they were speeding over
Ingleside, toward the Golden Gate Bridge through the crisp,
starry night.